W9-CKE-230

Crossing Delancey

Susan Sandler

A SAMUEL FRENCH ACTING EDITION

SAMUEL
FRENCH
FOUNDED 1830

SAMUELFRENCH.COM
SAMUELFRENCH-LONDON.CO.UK

Copyright © 1984, 1987 by Susan Sandler
All Rights Reserved

CROSSING DELANCEY is fully protected under the copyright laws of the
United States of America, the British Commonwealth, including Canada,
and all other countries of the Copyright Union. All rights, including professional and amateur stage productions, recitation, lecturing, public
reading, motion picture, radio broadcasting, television and the rights of
translation into foreign languages are strictly reserved.

ISBN 978-0-573-61988-5

www.SamuelFrench.com
www.SamuelFrench-London.co.uk

FOR PRODUCTION ENQUIRIES

UNITED STATES AND CANADA
Info@SamuelFrench.com
1-866-598-8449

UNITED KINGDOM AND EUROPE
Plays@SamuelFrench-London.co.uk
020-7255-4302

Each title is subject to availability from Samuel French, depending upon
country of performance. Please be aware that *CROSSING DELANCEY*
may not be licensed by Samuel French in your territory. Professional
and amateur producers should contact the nearest Samuel French
office or licensing partner to verify availability.

CAUTION: Professional and amateur producers are hereby warned that
CROSSING DELANCEY is subject to a licensing fee. Publication of this
play(s) does not imply availability for performance. Both amateurs and
professionals considering a production are strongly advised to apply to
Samuel French before starting rehearsals, advertising, or booking a theatre. A licensing fee must be paid whether the title(s) is presented for
charity or gain and whether or not admission is charged. Professional/
Stock licensing fees are quoted upon application to Samuel French.

No one shall make any changes in this title(s) for the purpose of
production. No part of this book may be reproduced, stored in a retrieval
system, or transmitted in any form, by any means, now known or yet to
be invented, including mechanical, electronic, photocopying, recording,
videotaping, or otherwise, without the prior written permission of the
publisher. No one shall upload this title(s), or part of this title(s), to any
social media websites.

For all enquiries regarding motion picture, television, and other media
rights, please contact Samuel French.

MUSIC USE NOTE

Licensees are solely responsible for obtaining formal written permission from copyright owners to use copyrighted music in the performance of this play and are strongly cautioned to do so. If no such permission is obtained by the licensee, then the licensee must use only original music that the licensee owns and controls. Licensees are solely responsible and liable for all music clearances and shall indemnify the copyright owners of the play(s) and their licensing agent, Samuel French, against any costs, expenses, losses and liabilities arising from the use of music by licensees. Please contact the appropriate music licensing authority in your territory for the rights to any incidental music.

IMPORTANT BILLING AND CREDIT REQUIREMENTS

If you have obtained performance rights to this title, please refer to your licensing agreement for important billing and credit requirements.

IMPORTANT ADVERTISING NOTE

ALL producers of CROSSING DELANCEY shall announce the name of Susan Sandler as the author of the play in all programs distributed in connection with performances of the play as hereinafter set forth, and in all instances in which the title of the play appears for the purposes of advertising, publicizing or otherwise exploiting the play and/or a production thereof, the name of Susan Sandler must also appear on a separate line on which no other name appears, immediately beneath the title, and must appear in size of type not less than Fifty Per Cent (50%) the size ot the title type.

IN ADDITION, producers must give the following acknowledgement on the first page of credits in all programs distributed in connection with performances of the play:

CROSSING DELANCEY
Originally produced by
the Jewish Repertory Theatre.

To Rose and Morris Sandler,
Nathan Eidels and, of course,
the one and only Sylvia Eidels

First preview: April 13, 1985
Opening night: April 25, 1985

THE JEWISH REPERTORY THEATRE
Ran Avni, Artistic Director • Edward M. Cohen, Associate Director

presents

CROSSING DELANCEY

a new play by
SUSAN SANDLER

directed by
PAMELA BERLIN

CAST
(In Order Of Appearance)

Isabelle	MELANIE MAYRON
Bubbie	SYLVIA KAUDERS
Hannah	SHIRLEY STOLER
Tyler	GEOFFREY PIERSON
Sam	JACOB HARRAN

Set Design by	Costume Design by	Lighting Design by
JEFFREY SCHNEIDER	LINDSAY DAVIS	BENNET AVERYT

Music by	Production Stage Manager
ROBERT DENNIS	ALICE DEWEY

The Time: the present.
The Place: New York City.

There will be one intermission.

CHARACTERS

BUBBIE — a fiesty, sharp-witted woman in her eighties, who immigrated to the United States as a young girl and has lived ever since in the shrinking community of New York City known as the lower east side.

ISABELLE — "Izzy" Grossman, her granddaughter, in her late twenties, a bookish dreamer.

HANNAH — a very large woman in her fifties, a professional matchmaker, a wheeler-dealer.

TYLER — a well known writer of fiction, handsome, exceedingly charming and self-involved, in his early forties.

SAM — a pickleman and a poet, an inhabitant of the lower east side, in his early thirties, gentle, intuitive, appealing, and very wise for his years.

TIME

The present

PLACE

New York City

A NOTE ABOUT STYLE AND MUSIC

The three basic areas of the play: Bubbie's kitchen, the bookstore, and the bench (which also doubles as Tyler's home for the phone conversation) are seen as islands that are easily traversed. Isabelle travels from one to the other while talking to us (in the monologues and with overlapping dialogue from one scene into the next.) There should be a complete fluidity of movement from one area to another, one scene to another, in a style that is almost filmic in rhythm.

A very important element in the design of this rhythm in the original production is the music composed for the play by Robert Dennis. It serves as the vivid transitional binding to the play's different worlds and supports the momentum of the shorter scenes and monologues. For information on the licensing of this music, please write or phone:

Robert Dennis
885 West End Ave., Apt. 3A
New York, N.Y. 10025
(212) 662-7242

— Susan Sandler

CROSSING DELANCEY

ACT I

An old woman is seated in an arm chair, a standing lamp pulled close, her head bent back in the hard light from the lamp. We see the back of a young woman, her feet sliding back and forth, trying to get a steady stance. She holds a metal tool in her hand. Her fingers caress the old woman's chin. The woman turns her head away, the tweezers fall to the floor.

Izzy. Hold still.
Bubbie. You're killing me.
Izzy. You want me to do it?
Bubbie. You don't have to kill me.
Izzy. Just hold still. One more. *(She pulls.)*
Bubbie. *(crying out)* OY!
Izzy. Okay.
Bubbie. Is that it?
Izzy. Yeah, I think so.
Bubbie. You sure?
Izzy. Yeah.
Bubbie. Be sure. You want me to run around like an old lady with a beard?
Izzy. Well, I do see a few more. Little ones.
Bubbie. So?

Izzy. You want me to do them?

Bubbie. What else? *(pause)* Pull. *Pull*

Izzy. Just two more. *(She fixes the tweezers delicately and yanks.)*

Bubbie. AH! You're killing me! *(Cries out again.)* Okay. Okay. Stop already. *(ISABELLE backs away and we see BUBBIE'S weathered face, beaming, proud.)* How do I look?

Izzy. Beautiful.

(Lights change to a spotlight on ISABELLE and BUBBIE who freezes on her last line.)

Izzy. *(Walks downstage from BUBBIE.)* That's my Bubbie. I visit her every Sunday. She sits in her special place, on her stool by the window. *Her* window. *(BUBBIE crosses down left to window area.)* I stand beside her, looking out at the East River below. She rubs my back. She holds me. I listen to her breathe. I love the smell of coffee on her breath. *(ISABELLE crosses to window, leans into the frame, BUBBIE rubs her back. They watch the life on the street.)* Bubbie?

Bubbie. Vas?

Izzy. Listen to this one — I'm in the ocean and the water has a funny color .... maybe pink or something. Maybe like somebody bled there recently — and I'm standing up. Not swimming. Not floating — I'm standing up and it's up to here on me — and the next thing I know the water level drops —— way down to here.

Bubbie. *(between gulps of coffee and bread)* It's good luck. Water is good luck.

Izzy. But what happens next is .... I walk out towards

the beach and when I turn around and look back at the ocean, it's all red .... this deep, deep red.

BUBBIE. Red is a very lucky color. It's good. It's good. You're gonna find money. Something good. *(She rises and picks up her dress, revealing another one underneath the first. She lifts that dress, then the first slip, followed by the second slip. In the middle of the second slip is a large, crudely sewn pocket which is sealed with three safety pins. She removes the pins and pulls from the pocket a large change purse. She opens it and produces a huge roll of bills. Her eyes shine as she fans the money out before ISABELLE.)* Such a lousy bundle of old paper I'm carrying. *(She peels off several bills and shoves them into ISABELLE's hand.)* Here. It's too heavy.

IzzY. Bubbie.

BUBBIE. Give me a break, help me out. Take a load off my back.

IzzY. Bubbie, this is five hundred dollars.

BUBBIE. Oh, yeah? That's all?

IzzY. Where did you get this?

BUBBIE. You saw.

IzzY. You're carrying this around? What about a bank?

BUBBIE. I like this. This I like. *(She lifts her skirt and pats her hidden pocket.)* This is my bank. This I trust.

IzzY. You just gave me five hundred dollars.

BUBBIE. So?

IzzY. For what?

BUBBIE. Do I need a reason to give my grandchild a little something? — You did a good job, you get paid for it. A hundred dollars for each whisker you pull. — A good price?

Izzy. A good price. *(She kisses her.)*

Bubbie. Come. Come to the table. Maybe I'll give you a crumb. *(They cross to the kitchen table. It is covered with platters of blintzes, sour cream in a large container, an old fashioned napkin holder jammed full of unironed and hastily folded napkins, mismatched china, bread, jars of homemade jam, etc...)*

Izzy. *(stabbing a blintze)* Do you think about your dreams, Bubbie?

Bubbie. Dreams is dreams. I see things. I get visits. Sometimes my Mama, sometimes my Papa. Last night my brother Nathan.

Izzy. Yeah?

Bubbie. He stopped by to say hello.

Izzy. Which one is Nathan?

Bubbie. Nathan, Nathan, the big inventor.

Izzy. Oh, right. Right.

Bubbie. A good man, a sweet man. He brought all of us here to this country. All fourteen children. And Mama and Papa. All of us. There never was a better brother. — But such an idiot.

Izzy. Tell me the story.

Bubbie. I told you already.

Izzy. Tell me again.

Bubbie. *(She settles down at the table.)* I was maybe twenty two, twenty three ... a real beauty, already married three years. I'm working in paper boxes and every Friday we go to Mama for dinner. A queen she was. Never lifted a finger for herself. Fourteen children to do for her. We worshipped her. A queen, I'm telling you.

Izzy. Nathan lived with her?

Bubbie. No, he put her in a fancy apartment. He

brought her over and put her in a lovely place. A palace.

Izzy. He was a good son.

Bubbie. The best. *(She gulps coffee and dunks some bread.)* So one afternoon we're having dinner. Nathan comes over and shows us some papers. He made up a plan to take the copper out of the ground and make it pure. Very cheap. The idea alone is worth a million bucks. Some skunk finds out he's a greenhorn ..... so what do they do? — They get him drunk, they make him sign papers in English that say he don't own no plans — *they* own the plans. — The next Sunday, he comes over for dinner. He eats a nice big bowl of soup, he kisses Mama, he kisses Papa's hand .... We're all talking, eating ... He goes into the bedroom ... BOOM! An explosion. I walk in, there's Nathan in the chair like this ... his eyeball hanging down on a string. A *yo-yo.* I walk over, I look at the gun, I look at Nathan and I spit on him. "PTU! PTU! Stupid idiot. Stupid stupid."

Izzy. Not everybody is as strong as you, Bubbie.

Bubbie. You said it. Look at this. *(She rolls up her sleeve and flexes her muscle. It dances as the flesh around it jiggles.)* This is me! *(BUBBIE closes her eyes and throws back her head and sings a full chorus of an old Russian folksong ... Then she dances around the kitchen, arms raised above her head, humming the next chorus.)* *

Izzy. *(applauds)* Bubbie, you should go on the stage.

Bubbie. I am on the stage. The whole East Side is my stage.

Izzy. *(Starts to collect her things.)* Anything else you want me to do before I go?

* See page 85.

BUBBIE. What? You going already? *(She looks toward the window.)* Yes... it's dark... go. Go. You'll call me when you get home. — Ah — it's a terrible, terrible thing. Terrible.

IZZY. What?

BUBBIE. That you should be all alone. — A professor once said. A college professor. No matter how much money you got, if you're alone, you're sick.

IZZY. I'm not alone.

BUBBIE. You took in a borderka?

IZZY. No, but I have friends, people at the bookstore — I'm not alone.

BUBBIE. All day you stand in a bookstore ... you make your room a bookstore .... Books don't make blintzes, my girl ... books is just paper. Books can't be your Bubbie. Books can't be your husband.

IZZY. Bubbie, please don't start—

BUBBIE. You listen to me, loneliness is a very lousy case. I sit in the house when you go away. I sit and one day, I listen, I'm talkin' to myself. Plain, I thought I was meshugah. Talkin' and makin' with my hands and talkin'. That's how you get nervous.

IZZY. I'll see you next week. *(She kisses her.)*

BUBBIE. *(tying a kerchief around her head)* Call me. Let me know that you're safe. Don't talk to nobody. The subways are murder. Be smart. Call me. I'm waiting. *(IZZY opens the door.)* I don't breathe until I hear that phone.

(Crossfade to the bookstore. Phone rings in bookstore.)

IZZY. *(Finds her keys in her bag and opens the door, rushing to pick up the ringing phone.)* New Day Books. — Yes, what's the name? — Oh, hi. Yes, just a minute, let me check — *(She holds the phone to her chest.)* It's Tyler Moss! — *(pause)* You think you've never heard of him, but you have — FREEFALL, CONFESSIONS OF A CAVE DWELLER, SKIRT TALES — I've got them all. First editions. Signed. — I even have a videotape of his appearance on "Book Ends". Remember "Book Ends"? Back in '83 — with Rupert Clark? On Channel 13? — Rupert asks Tyler what his work routine is like and Tyler says, "The only thing I do *routinely* is breathe." — He comes into the shop here a couple of times a week to buy some specialty periodicals and to check the sales on his books. — We've never had much conversation. Nothing more than the grim numbers on his sales — I don't know why his last book never moved, but I usually have to say we're well stocked. That's how I put it. So there isn't much chance for me to open things up ..... but there is this ... *undercurrent.* I can feel it. He gives it away with his eyes. They're grey blue and very very smokey and mysterious. When I hand him back his change and he looks down to count it — I give each of his eyelids a secret kiss. *(She brings the phone back to her ear.)* No, I'm sorry — it's not in yet. Should be here by Wednesday. At the very latest. I'll save one for you. — Anytime, Mr. Moss. Just ask for Isabelle. —Right.

(Lights up on BUBBIE, approaching the park bench.)

BUBBIE. Isabelle! Come here! Here .... sit here. Not where those koot-sehs can give you their bad eyes. Their eyes should twist into their heads, those pas-kootz-vahs.

(She spits. IZZY gathers up her bag and crosses to her from the store. They settle down on the bench and look around the park.)
Pull your dress down.

Izzy. It is down.

Bubbie. Naked legs. What can I do? *(BUBBIE looks around the park and swings her legs back and forth happily.)* Don't scream.

Izzy. Why should I scream?

Bubbie. Hannah's coming.

Izzy. Who?

Bubbie. Hannah. She's coming over.

Izzy. Yeah?

Bubbie. I asked her to say hello.

Izzy. I don't think I know her.

Bubbie. I made her some tagelah. *(She pulls out a coffee jar full of honeyed balls of dough.)* She loves my tagelah. Who wouldn't? She's never tasted anything so good in her whole life.

Izzy. Why should I scream?

Bubbie. Once I gave her some blintzes. I made a mistake — I let her come in the house. I sat her down. I gave her coffee. I gave her blintzes. Blueberry. Cheese. You name it. She couldn't eat fast enough. A regular garbage truck.

Izzy. *Why should I scream?*

Bubbie. Hannah. *Hannah.* The shadkhn.

Izzy. You made an appointment with a marriage broker?!

Bubbie. She's had her eye on you for a long time.

Izzy. Wait a minute—

Bubbie. Everytime you come to visit. You go away, she

comes over, she says to me, Ida, Ida, what is going to happen to that girl? What can I tell her. You live alone in a room. Like a dog. A dog should live alone. Not people. A dog. Loneliness is a sickness. I should know. Loneliness is a sickness all by itself.

Izzy. It is not a *room*. It's an apartment. A very nice apartment. You've been there. You know. There's a bedroom and a bathroom and a little kitchen and lots of furniture. It's not a room.

Bubbie. With bars on the windows like a prison. Someone should crawl in at night I'm always thinking.

Izzy. Stop thinking.

Bubbie. Why not? I gotta think. I wait for you, you'll never do it.

Izzy. What are you talking about?

Bubbie. *You.* I'm talking about you. — She's got some nice boys. Some fine, respectable boys. Not like Nate the butcher. His mother is a spider. Feh! — Oh, he has some big eye out for you. Whenever you go to buy meat with me, he gives me a little something extra, always on the side a few ounces. I see him do it. He knows. I watch him.

Izzy. Bubbie, this isn't the way I live. This is a hundred years ago. This isn't me.

Bubbie. You can say that again.

(HANNAH, a very large woman, waddles towards them around the circle of benches, stopping to shake hands and chat.)

Bubbie. Listen, to *her* you're a prize. A jewel. — A little bit old, maybe, but you're mine. You're a million bucks.

Don't worry.

HANNAH. *(Her fleshy face is suddenly bent close into BUBBIE and IZZY.)* Ida! Idaela!

BUBBIE. This is it. This is mine ainical.

HANNAH. Yes. She's a beauty.

BUBBIE. Ain't she a beauty? PTU! PTU! PTU! *(She spits three times.)*

IZZY. Excuse me, but I don't know—

BUBBIE. *(interrupting her)* First you'll listen, then you'll talk.

HANNAH. *(sitting next to IZZY, sandwiching her in with BUBBIE on the other end)* Very nice. Very nice girl. *(She pats IZZY's hands.)* She lives by her parents?

BUBBIE. No, they live in Florida. With Red Buttons. All the alta cockers under one roof. You can have it.

HANNAH. She's lucky she's got her Bubbie to take care of her.

BUBBIE. You said it.

HANNAH. So, Isabelle, you got your own apartment?

BUBBIE. *(before IZZY can respond)* Yeah, two fifty a month, gas and electric. A room with a kitchen. Like a dog.

HANNAH. Well, this can change. She's a lovely girl. She opens her eyes, she looks around, she meets a fellah. With a little help, ahah?

BUBBIE. *(Pulls out the jar of tagelah from her bag and offers it to HANNAH.)* Hannah. For you. Something nice.

HANNAH. *(Accepts the jar, opens it, takes one piece out, pops the large, sticky mass into her mouth and with lips smacking, smiles broadly into IZZY's face.)* Deeeee-licious!!

(Crossfade to bookstore. IZZY crosses into bookstore and stands behind the counter, burying her head in a book. TYLER MOSS enters.)

TYLER. *(studying her silently, then:)* You must get a lot of reading done here.

IZZY. *(looking up from the book, startled)* Oh — Hi.

TYLER. I hope I haven't stopped you at a crucial moment.

IZZY. Oh — no.

TYLER. I remember back in school when I worked in the bookstore, if I really got into something I would go hide in the back room so I could finish a chapter without getting interrupted.

IZZY. We don't have much of a backroom.

TYLER. You don't seem to have much business either.... *(He looks around the store.)* How are things going?

IZZY. Fine. Fine. — We're well stocked on all your books. — We do our best to keep neighborhood authors prominently displayed — See, you're still out there—*(She points to the window.)*

TYLER. Yeah — *(looking over to the window)* — Looks a little yellow, doesn't it? — But I am going to have something new coming out — in the fall. I'll give you plenty of advance notice on it ... in case you want to do something special with the window.

IZZY. I'm sure we will. — Can I help you with anything today?

TYLER. I came in for the *Paris Review.*

IZZY. Not in yet.

TYLER. Yes, I noticed. Sorry to have interrupted your reading.

IZZY. No problem. — I've read it before.

TYLER. Oh? — *(He crosses back to her.)* Second reads can be the sweetest — like lots of things on the second tasting —What is it? *(She turns the book up, revealing the cover of his novel, FREEFALL.)*

IZZY. *(smiling shyly)* Actually, it's my third read.

TYLER. This is called adrenalin to the ego — my god — your *third!* It's not *that* good.

IZZY. Oh it is ... it is.

TYLER. Well ... thank you. Thank you very much. — I'm all mush-mouth — I don't know what to say .... Can I sign it for you?

IZZY. You already have. I got it the day you were here signing books. Just after it came out.

TYLER. *(picking up the book and looking inside the cover)* But — there's no inscription. That won't do — *(taking his pen from his pocket)* Please forgive me, I've forgotten your name.

IZZY. Isabelle Grossman. — *Izzy mostly.*

TYLER. Izzy — I like it. *(Holds the book and closes his eyes trying to think of something to write.)* My god, I can't think straight — I'm still swooning from your compliment — Okay, let's see. *(He starts to write. IZZY is glowing. He hands her back the book.)*

IZZY. Thanks, Mr. Moss.

TYLER. Tyler, please.

IZZY. Thanks, Ty.

TYLER. Just Tyler. *(Walks to the door.)* My deepest pleasure. *(exits)*

Izzy. *(Opens book and reads inscription.)* To Izzy, A reader's devotion is a writer's nourishment. Thanks for the meal. Always, Tyler Moss. *(She closes the book and kisses the jacket.)*

(Crossfade to kitchen. BUBBIE stands ironing at the kitchen table. She uses a very old, heavy iron that she slams down for emphasis as she talks. IZZY crosses left to her.)

Bubbie. The important thing is you shouldn't go naked.

Izzy. I'm not going at all.

Bubbie. You're going, you're going. But not naked. Not like that. You put on a nice dress. You put on stockings. You look like a person. No naked legs.

Izzy. Bubbie, you don't understand, I can't do this.

Bubbie. Hannah says he's the best she's got. — That pickle stand on Ludlow — that's him. That's some nice business.

Izzy. What can I say to a pickleman?

Bubbie. You're over twenty-one. — His father just died last year. He's the oldest, so it's his business naturally. She says there's a younger brother, Moishe — not much there. Sam is the one for you. — We'll see. We'll take a look.

Izzy. I can't believe you're doing this.

Bubbie. If I waited for your mother to do something for you I'd die without any great-grandchildren. — What kind of life do you have alone in that room? What is that?

Izzy. Bubbie, it's very different for women of my

generation. It's not like it was for you. Everything's different. We have options.

BUBBIE. Options? What's options?

IZZY. Like choices — like you don't have to do things the same way other people do. — It's a tremendous luxury I have. — I can do anything I want to do. Go anywhere I want to go.

BUBBIE. Tell me the truth, you ever go out with a boy sometime?

IZZY. Sometimes ... sure. I have — plenty. — I have plenty of boyfriends.

BUBBIE. Plenty? You don't need plenty. You need only *one*. Who you got? I don't see nobody.

IZZY. I haven't brought them to meet you yet — they're friends — you know. Nothing serious yet.

BUBBIE. Listen, my girl .... friends is friends ... and you can do *this* with them. *(She makes an obscene gesture.)* A husband is a husband for life.

IZZY. Maybe I don't want a husband.

BUBBIE. *(slamming the iron down)* Don't talk crazy.

IZZY. And if I did, he wouldn't be a pickleman.

BUBBIE. Get off your high horse, Miss Universe .... this man is just lookin' ..... He ain't askin' to buy.

(Crossfade to center bench area and bookstore as IZZY crosses down.)

IZZY. Sometimes I think if he could see me *outside* the store — it would all be different. He would be able to think of me in an entirely different context .... That's all it really is — is context. Right now I'm just his girl behind the counter. Oh, I read his books and I am clearly an admirer. That much he knows.... But he hasn't seen me. — Not yet he hasn't. *(She crosses into bookstore and picks up copy of TYLER's book, Freefall)* His bio reads, "Tyler Moss lives in New York City with his collection of early American photography and his two cats, Scott and Zelda." — Pretty encouraging, don't you think?

(Lights change to dreamy hot pinks and reds as TYLER enters the store.)

TYLER. *(spotting the copy of Freefall ISABELLE still holds)* Not again — this is too much ... You're on your fourth read!? You'll make the Guiness Book of Records.

Izzy. No .... no, I was just putting it in my bag to take back home.

TYLER. Good.

Izzy. The *Paris Review*'s in.

TYLER. Yes, I see.

Izzy. So's *Rivers* — something wrong? *(silence)* Did I say something wrong?

TYLER. You look different ... you're not wearing your glasses.

Izzy. I've got my contacts in.

TYLER. *(moving closer)* There's something else—

Izzy. Is it my hair?

TYLER. It's shimmering ... it's almost — maybe it's the light but — it almost looks like a halo.

Izzy. Could be the henna rinse.

TYLER. And there's something else— *(Moves still closer.)* Your mouth — it's softer ... painfully sweet and—

Izzy. Kissable?

Tyler. Yes.

Izzy. I've been waiting for this, Tyler.

Tyler. Have you?

Izzy. I've been waiting for you to notice me.

Tyler. I've always noticed you. Why do you think I make so many excuses to come into this store? Why do you think I haunt these shelves? Do you really think I'm checking on the sales of my books? — Nonsense — it's *you*, Izzy.

Izzy. Oh, Ty.

Tyler. Just Tyler. *(scooping her up in his arms)* Come on, let's make sense of our lives — let's forget the courting rituals... I know who you are Isabelle Grossman... and I want you in my life. *(Places her back on the counter, extending his arms out to her. IZZY leaps from the counter, falling to the floor.)*

(Lights brighten noticeably as TYLER reenters.)

Tyler. *(helping her up)* This is what comes from reading too much — you lose your traveling vision — Hey, don't I remember seeing you in glasses? Don't you wear glasses?

Izzy. Yes... but I've got my contacts in. *(brushing herself off)* Thanks.

Tyler. You okay?

Izzy. Fine... I'm fine. Gotta get this area cleared up, I guess. *(regaining her composure)* Can I help you with something?

Tyler. You sure you're okay? You look a little out

of sorts.

Izzy. Just over-worked.

Tyler. Put this one on my account, will you? *(Takes magazine.)* I'm a little short today ... and I'm sorry, please forgive me. I've forgotten your name—

Izzy. Isabelle. But you can call me Izzy.

Tyler. Yes ... *Izzy,* That's right. Of course. Well, thanks, Izzy .... and give those eyes a rest. *(He exits.)*

(Crossfade to BUBBIE's kitchen. IZZY crosses left as the lights come up in BUBBIE's kitchen. HANNAH, SAM and ISABELLE sit at the table. BUBBIE stands at the stove, pouring water into three tea cups.)

Hannah. *(Holds up an old photograph backed with cardboard and taped at the edges.)* This is you, Ida?

Bubbie. In the middle.

Hannah. This one?

Bubbie. *(grabbing the picture from her)* Here. *This* one. — Look at your hands. Be a person. Use a napkin.

Hannah. Excuse me.

Bubbie. *(pointing out the figure in the photo)* That's the one. That's the girl ... Twenty-one years old. Cheeks like apples. They fought like cats and dogs for me. I got rings, big chocolate cakes from the fanciest bakeries they brought to my mother. I looked, I listened. They all had the same song and dance. They all wanted sweet Idela. They all wanted me.

Hannah. *(pointing to another figure in the photo)* And this one?

Bubbie. My sister, Bessie. She was the quiet one. She

didn't know how to open her mouth.

HANNAH. She's still alive, yes?

BUBBIE. Yeah, she lives in Jersey. We don't see each other for fifteen years maybe.

HANNAH. How come?

BUBBIE. She learned how to open her mouth. *(BUBBIE serves the tea.)*

SAM. Mrs. Kantor.

BUBBIE. What?

SAM. Would you mind, in a glass please?

BUBBIE. In a glass. Like a good Russian boy. Certainly, certainly. A glass for the pickleman. *(She transfers the tea to a glass.)*

HANNAH. *(Smiles approvingly.)* Ain't he something. He's new, he's fresh. He likes the modern way, but he understands what's good. Right, Sam?

SAM. Right.

BUBBIE. You like my blintzes?

SAM. They're very good, Mrs. Kantor.

BUBBIE. They're the best thing you ever put in your mouth! Isabelle. Isabelle! You gonna push or you gonna eat?

IZZY. I'm not so hungry, Bubbie.

BUBBIE. Since when?

HANNAH. Leave her alone, Idela. — So, Sam, talk to us. Give us the picture, yes?

SAM. Well, Mrs. Mandelbaum .... I don't know. What do you want to know?

HANNAH. Your future, your plans, your thoughts, what you dream about, what you do with yourself. Anything.

SAM. *(laughing nervously)* Well, uh ... I'm a pretty happy fella, you know. I like to get up in the morning and hear the birds tweet-tweet. I put on a nice clean shirt. I walk to shule and make the morning prayers. I have a cup coffee by my friend Schlomo's. Then nine o'clock my doors open. — It begins! — You make good blintzes, Mrs. Kantor, but I got to tell you, I make the best pickles in New York.

BUBBIE. Is that so?

SAM. That is so. And to prove it, I brought you a present. The best I got. *(He pulls out a series of jars from a shopping bag at his side.)* You got sour and half sour and here's a little kraut which you also cannot beat. And some sweet little baby tomatoes. *(He has lined the merchandise up on the table.)*

BUBBIE. *(Goes to the table and holds up the jar of pickles to the light.)* Looks nice. I got to tell you something, Sam. I been buyin' pickles from Hiam for 30 years maybe, so don't hold it against me.

SAM. I look at it this way, Mrs. Kantor, whatever happens between us, I'm doing you a favor giving you my pickles. You been missing the best.

HANNAH. He knows what's what. This is confidence.

BUBBIE. So what you got to say for yourself, Isabelle?

IZZY. Excuse me?

HANNAH. *(getting up)* Idela, I got to peek at those drapes in the living room. You gonna show me how you make them so nice?

BUBBIE. What are you talkin'?

HANNAH. *(taking her by the elbow)* Come, come.

BUBBIE. I can walk by myself very nicely, thank you. *(They exit. SAM and IZZY sit silently at the table. IZZY stares down at her plate. She has not looked directly at SAM during the entire interview.)*

SAM. I like a quiet girl.

IZZY. That's nice.

SAM. And softspoken, too. *(pulling his chair in closer to her)* That's some Bubbie you got.

IZZY. Yeah.

SAM. She's a corker.

IZZY. Yeah.

SAM. You come to visit every Sunday?

IZZY. Yeah.

SAM. I think she loves you very much.

IZZY. *(pause)* Listen — *(looking up for the first time)*

SAM. Yes?

IZZY. I didn't have anything to do with this. It wasn't my idea.

SAM. You feel funny, huh?

IZZY. This isn't the way I live. This isn't the way I do things.

SAM. How *do* you live?

IZZY. Well, for one thing, I don't live down here.

SAM. Yes?

IZZY. I live uptown.

SAM. Is that right?

IZZY. Yes, and emotionally — sociologically, I'm a million miles from here.

SAM. This isn't your style.

IZZY. This *isn't* my style.

SAM. Sometimes you can change your style.

Izzy. You don't understand—

Sam. Sometimes you put on a new hat, you become a new person.

Izzy. Look, I'm sorry you had to go through all this, but when my Bubbie wants something—

Sam. I have a friend, Harry Shipman. Shipman Imports. Lox, caviar, fancy stuff. For years he wore the same kind of hat. A little brown cap, the brim pulled down, you wondered how he could see. One day, he's crossing Delancey, a big wind comes — poof— it's gone. He runs after it, but it's too late, a truck gets there before he does. He comes into me, crying, he feels so bad. I said, Harry. Harry, I said, here. Here's a present. From me to you. Take five dollars, go across to Finkle, buy yourself a new one, something special. From me to you. But do me a favor, forget the brown cap. He goes, he picks out, he comes back an hour later. He's a new man. *A grey felt Stetson!* A beauty! The next day he makes an engagement.

Izzy. To be married?

Sam. That's right. — Between you and me he must of given him some Nova on the side. — That's no five-dollar hat.

Izzy. A man trades some lox for a Stetson and gets a bride in the bargain. Very romantic.

Sam. Oh, he had his eye on her for a long time. But she couldn't see him. The cap. That little brown cap. She couldn't see his eyes. *(He bends down close and stares into her eyes. IZZY tries to look away, but feels herself drawn into the warm, bright, steady gaze.)*

(BUBBIE bursts into the kitchen, HANNAH trailing behind.)

BUBBIE. *(over her shoulder to HANNAH)* What are you hocking me a chineick?

HANNAH. It's nice to *know* these things.

BUBBIE. So, children, what's new?

HANNAH. *(settling down at the table)* Maybe a little more tea, Ida?

BUBBIE. Sam, what's the story?

SAM. You got a sweet girl here, Mrs. Kantor.

BUBBIE. Ach! She's a mean, nasty, stinkin' little brat— *(She plants a big, sopping kiss on IZZY's cheek)* But she's mine. What you gonna do?!

HANNAH. You got a little hot water over there?

BUBBIE. Henka, Henka, give your mouth a rest, it will thank you. *(to SAM)* So, what's the plan?

HANNAH. You forgot, Ida, why *I'm* here?

BUBBIE. I don't forget.

HANNAH. Then maybe you'll let me do my job.

BUBBIE. I see two beautiful children sitting at my table, enjoying my cooking. What's the job?

HANNAH. I give up.

BUBBIE. Good. Sam?

SAM. Well, I thought Saturday night maybe I could take Isabelle to supper at Sammy's Roumanian.

HANNAH. Oh, are you gonna *EAT!*

BUBBIE. You'll pick her up six o'clock sharp, she'll be back by ten. You'll stay over by me, Isabelle, no running in taxis.

SAM. *(to IZZY)* Is that okay? Would you like that? It's a very nice place.

BUBBIE. She'll like, she'll like.

IZZY. Thank you, but I don't think so.

Bubbie. What's this?

Izzy. It's been lovely meeting you, Sam, and I appreciate your kind invitation, but I don't think I want to go. Thank you very much.

Bubbie. *(pause)* Well. She spoke.

Hannah. You look, you meet, you try, you see. Sometimes it fits, sometimes it don't.

Bubbie. She spoke.

Sam. *(rising)* Thank you, Mrs. Kantor, for the exceptional blintzes.

Bubbie. The *best.*

Sam. Yes. *(He collects his hat and shopping bag.)* Mrs. Mandelbaum.

Hannah. Zi ge zunt, Sam.

Sam. Zi ge zunt. *(He starts for the door and turns.)* Isabelle. You should try a new hat sometime. It might look good on you. *(IZZY and SAM lock stares for a brief moment. Then she pulls her eyes away. His hand touches the doorknob. Blackout.)*

(IZZY crosses down left in a single spot.)

Izzy. Last night I got my nerve up and called. I got his unlisted home number from the files at the store. That part was easy. The hard part was figuring out what I would say — I wanted to catch him off guard, but not sound too kooky or desperate. I wanted to peel back the careful layers of polite conversation and let him say what I hoped was really on his mind — in his heart. In other words — this was to be an *ambush. (She picks up the phone and dials.)*

(We hear ringing. Then the ringing stops. Lights up on TYLER holding the phone. He wears a towel. IZZY shuffles several 3x5 cards.)

TYLER. Hello.

IZZY. Tyler?

TYLER. Yes.

IZZY. Izzy.

TYLER. I beg your pardon?

IZZY. Izzy Grossman. Isabelle Grossman. From New Day Books. *(pause)* The girl at the downstairs counter who sometimes wears contacts and sometimes wears glasses — who tripped as you were coming into the store this week — who's read *FREEFALL* more times than you want to know—

TYLER. Oh, yes, yes. Isabelle.

IZZY. Or Izzy.

TYLER. Izzy — yes. *(pause)* Well — what's up? Am I in terrible debt over there? I know I owe some money, but isn't this kind of bad form, calling folks at ten at night to collect bills? You know I'm good for it.

IZZY. I'm not calling on store business.

TYLER. Oh?

IZZY. *(reading from one of the cards)* I'm calling to give you a chance to express yourself more freely outside the confines of our formal friendship. *(Tosses card away.)*

TYLER. I didn't realize we had a formal friendship.

IZZY. *(reading from another card)* The work-a-day world does frame our contact. — I want to give you a chance to crawl out of that frame.

TYLER. Well, right now I've just crawled out of the shower and I'm standing here dripping—

Izzy. Oh, I'm sorry.

TYLER. I'm also working pretty furiously on a review that's due in next week so my time is kinda tight. But if you like, maybe one day I could take you out for coffee and you can interview me. What is this for — graduate thesis?

Izzy. No ... just something I'm doing on my own.

TYLER. Small magazine? Straight Q and A I hope. Listen, I'll drop by next week, we'll set a time, you can bring a small tape recorder then prepare the *un*edited transcript. I get final edit. Those are my conditions. Okay?

Izzy. Yeah. That's great.

(Blackout. Lights up on center bench area where HANNAH sits fanning herself, her shoes off, a full shopping cart at her side. IZZY walks by without noticing her, absorbed in her thoughts.)

HANNAH. Isabelle, vus tuht seh?

Izzy. Oh. Hello, Mrs. Mandelbaum.

HANNAH. Come. Sit.

Izzy. I can't — Bubbie's expecting me.

HANNAH. Sit a minute. It wouldn't kill you.

Izzy. I don't like to keep her waiting.

HANNAH. *(a big smile on her face)* I got something for you.

Izzy. What?

HANNAH. Sit. A *minute*.

Izzy. *(sits)* What is it?

HANNAH. It's perfect. A little corsette shop on Orchard. They got a nice line in brassiers, too. I never bought nothing there, but it's good quality stuff. This

I know.

Izzy. Is this another—

Hannah. He's a little bit older than the pickleman, but a heart like this — on him. A *heart,* I'm telling you. — Every year he sends his mama to Miami Beach. Every year. And this one is a very smooth talker, not like the pickleman. This one can *talk.*

Izzy. Mrs. Mandelbaum, I don't know why you're doing this. I'm *not* interested.

Hannah. She's *not* interested. *(pause)* So when we gonna hear the bells?

Izzy. What bells?

Hannah. What bells .... the *marriage* bells — what else?

Izzy. What are you talking about?

Hannah. When a girl tells me she ain't interested in meeting some nice boys lookin' to marry that means only one thing — she's got it picked out. — So, who's the lucky fella? You gonna invite me, I hope. With a cook like your Bubbie, it's gonna be some *nash,* yes?

Izzy. *I'm not getting married.*

Hannah. No?

Izzy. No.

Hannah. So what's the matter with you? Why all the tzimis? — Take a chance, meet a fella. You're not gonna be a chicken forever.

Izzy. Excuse me, Mrs. Mandelbaum. *(She rises.)*

Hannah. A little advice from someone who knows what's good — Love comes and goes very quickly. A good business with a nice home, a man who knows his job, who's good and kind — *this* is what lasts. Everything else is cotton candy, my dear girl.

Izzy. Goodbye, Mrs. Mandelbaum.

Hannah. You listen to me — I know about life. From the inside out.

(Blackout. Lights up on BUBBIE who crosses to her stool, carrying a bottle of rubbing alcohol. She sits slowly, painfully.)

Bubbie. Right here it gets me. In the shoulder. — Nem. Nem. — Nem de alcohol. *(IZZY crosses to her and takes the rubbing alcohol, opens the bottle, pours some into her hands and rubs BUBBIE's shoulders.)* Ahh ... that's good. That's good...

Izzy. Too hard?

Bubbie. No ... no — it's good. It's like an angel — your hands. — Ach! This one is the killer. This is where it gets me. In the shoulder. — And the knees — the knees, too. *(IZZY rubs her gently.)* You put a little alcohol every day, you live to be a hundred tsvansig.

Izzy. You promise?

Bubbie. Ach, you're too young to worry for such things. All you worry for is to find the *prince* — ain't I right?

Izzy. I don't know.

Bubbie. I know what I'm talkin'. *(pause)* I pass the pickleman on Orchard yesterday. So nice and polite. And such sweet eyes on him. Your ainical, he says, she's a special one — That's right, I say, she comes from me, what else. *(as IZZY rubs)* Oh, that's good — that's good, right there. — Such a nice boy. — You mixed him up plenty, you murderer.

IZZY. Bubbie, I'm sorry — he's just not my type. I'm sorry.

BUBBIE. Sorry — sorry. Stop being so sorry. That's one word I hate.

IZZY. You've got to try and understand.

BUBBIE. Is it my fault if you don't know a good boy when you see one? Some people got eyes, some people don't.

IZZY. Bubbie, there's got to be something happening between two people. There's got to be — you know, like *heat.*

BUBBIE. I'll give you heat.

IZZY. And the other thing you should know is I'm going out with someone who looks like he might be very interested in me.

BUBBIE. You're keeping company with someone?

IZZY. *(hesitates)* —Y— yes. He's a writer. A very famous, wonderful writer.

BUBBIE. So what's cookin'?

IZZY. He can't stay away from me. He comes into the bookstore a couple times a week. Hangs around.

BUBBIE. You shouldn't lose your job from him.

IZZY. Oh, no. No, I won't. Don't worry.

BUBBIE. Once, I was selling cigars, cigarettes, penny candy, a little stand near Grand street. I was a girl, a killer, such a beauty. This poor schmendrick would come every day to look on me — he knew I was a married woman. This didn't stop him. He came, he bought cigars. He bought candy. He gave me a fancy ring.

IZZY. You took it?

BUBBIE. Sure I took it. He's got a right to give me. It's a

free country. He knew what was doing by me. — He was crazy in love, what can I tell you.

(The doorbell rings.)

BUBBIE. What's that?

IZZY. The bell.

BUBBIE. I know it's the bell.

IZZY. Well. Aren't you gonna answer?

BUBBIE. Naaaaa, it's those kids making monkey business. Animals. They should break their arms off. They pull the buttons off the elevators. Make marks on the walls. Like pigs. *(IZZY crosses to the door and looks through the peephole.)* Isabelle, get away from that door!

IZZY. *(through the door)* Who is it?

VOICE. Eastside Delivery Service.

IZZY. Show us your ID card. — Slip it under the door. *(She does. Holding it up for BUBBIE.)* See, it's the real thing.

BUBBIE. You open the door, it's goodbye, cookie, goodbye.

IZZY. *(Begins to unlock the door.)* Relax, Bubbie—

BUBBIE. *YOU HEAR ME!?!*

IZZY. *(Opens the door, takes the package, and signs the receipt.)* Thanks. *(She walks to the kitchen table, carrying the large package marked "Fragile." She takes a knife from the counter as she crosses with it. Smiling proudly.)* See. What did I tell you?

BUBBIE. It's the wrong person. They made a mistake. — What's it? What's in there?

IZZY. *(cutting the string)* We'll see, Bubbie.

BUBBIE. *(rushing to her, grabbing the knife away)* Gimme

that. Gimme that. You don't know how to open a package. That's good string you're wasting. I should know. I worked in paper boxes for five years. Look at these hands. When you open a package you go slow and easy. That's good paper, too. Look at this. Nice heavy paper. Something to save. And the string you don't throw out. Miss Fancy. You go so fast you cut it in a million pieces. Then what you got? Here. See? This is the way. Nice and easy does it. *(BUBBIE removes first a bakery box. Opening it, out comes a large, luscious, many-layered chocolate cake.)*

BUBBIE. Oy gevalt! Who's this? *(IZZY sees something else in the box and reaches in and pulls out another box.)* What's this? *(IZZY opens it and pulls out a sweet, grey felt Stetson. She runs her hands along the fabric ... Lets out a little gasp and rushes to the mirror where she puts it on at a rakish angle. It looks sensational.)* Who's this? What's going on?

IZZY. *(turning away from the mirror)* Bubbie ... I'm being woooooed.

BUBBIE. Woooed? Vas is wooooed?

(Blackout. Music up.)

END OF ACT I

ACT II

*BUBBIE'S apartment. SAM stands in the window frame, stretch-
ing up and out as far as his short body will allow. In his
hand he holds a long stick with a rag sealed to the end by
several layers of rubber bands. BUBBIE stands behind
him, watching.*

BUBBIE. In the corner. *(She bangs on the window.)*
SAM. What? *(He leans back into the room.)*
BUBBIE. In the corner, a little bit dirty. Just a touch.
SAM. Oh. Okay. *(He leans back out again, stretching still
further, and reaching the corner section of the window with the
stick. Then he slides back into the room.)* Gut?
BUBBIE. Zere gut. You should live a thousand years.
SAM. It's all my pleasure, Mrs. Kantor. It was a good
thing I came over. You shouldn't do this by yourself.
BUBBIE. Come, wash your hands. I'll give you a bite.
SAM. *(Crosses to the basin and rolls up his sleeves.)* No thanks
— I'm not hungry.
BUBBIE. You're too skinny, Sam. I see the bones.
SAM. I always eat a big breakfast after shule.
BUBBIE. You go to shule every morning?
SAM. Most days.
BUBBIE. I don't go to shule. I don't look for God. God
finds me.
SAM. I'm not a rabbi. I'm not a hassid. I go because I

like to speak the poetry. I like to sing the songs. It puts something sweet in my mouth.

BUBBIE. I'm gonna put something sweet in your mouth— *(crossing to the oven)* You're a lucky man, Sammy. You know what you smell? *(Opens oven.)* You're gonna cry from happiness. *(She removes a pan and holds it up for him to see.)* A kugel from heaven. *(Places the dish on the table, and begins to sing as she cuts the steaming casserole.)**

HUT A YID A YID-EH-NEH
HUT ERR FOON IRR TZORIS
MACHT TSEE OISS AH KIGALEH
TAIG ISS OFF KOPURISS
OIY MEIN MAHN, AH SAY FILL DIR MOKES
VIH FIL KER KIGALEH
COST MIR KOPAKAS

Ach! What a voice I got! On Suffolk Street you should have seen them. I would open the window and give a yell — Hey, Mr. Schwartz, I got something for you! — He lived across from me — then I'd sing — ofen pribitzik, der alta mahn, de kugeleh song — When I'm finished everybody is hanging from the windows — screaming for me. — Here, I'm up so high. In these projects it's nice, it's clean, but who can hear a person sing?

SAM. I feel honored to be your audience, Mrs. Kantor.

BUBBIE. I like you, Sam. You're a smart cookie. You got a few brains.

SAM. So .... I'm sure you didn't call me over to your house just to help you wash your windows, Mrs. Kantor.

BUBBIE. This is your busiest day, no? You can run away

* See page 85.

like this on your busiest day?

SAM. My brother and his friend, Pinkie, can take care of the store. Sometimes there are more important things than business.

BUBBIE. I'm sure you know what you're talking.... You like your work?

SAM. Very much. There was a time — when I was in college — I went for two years — I wasn't sure what I wanted to do. I wanted to study literature. My father said, whatever I wanted, fine. He never pushed me. — I thought I might be a teacher, a poet... You have these dreams when you're a child.

BUBBIE. I worked, I worked all my life. What else is there? In the depression you see the poor fellows out of work, hungry, tired from looking they come into the Horn & Hardart Cafeteria where I am cleaning the tables. My job is to walk around and pick up the trays, the dishes, after the customer finishes eating. The lucky ones who got a nickle to buy a bowl of soup, a quarter for a plate of corned beef, they eat what they want and leave over, you know? And at the next table somebody is looking like this— *(She makes a face.)* So what do I do? I walk around picking up here, putting down there. This way nothing is wasted. Everybody who comes in, goes away with something in his belly. This was a job.

SAM. *(Puts down his fork.)* So, Mrs. Kantor, tell me, did you receive the package?

BUBBIE. What kind?

SAM. It was a box — maybe this big — with a cake ... and — I didn't put a name inside. I thought—

BUBBIE. Oh, this was from *you*. Very nice, Sam. It must

have been 3 .... 4 eggs, half pound butter — good quality chocolate. Nothing cheap here.

SAM. Zalmen the baker made it for me. A special request.

BUBBIE. Very tasty. *(Points to his plate.)* You're not eating, Sam.

SAM. And the hat? Was Isabelle here? Did she see the hat?

BUBBIE. The hat?

SAM. There was a hat — inside.

BUBBIE. Ah, yes, yes. She looked at it.

SAM. Did she like it? Did she put it on?

BUBBIE. Vas?

SAM. *The hat.*

BUBBIE. Yeah — sure.

SAM. Thank you for the kugel, Mrs. Kantor. *(He gets up.)* I'm going back to my stand.

BUBBIE. Sam! — *(She motions for him to sit.)* Please. Sit down. *(He sits.)* Sammy, listen good. I'm gonna give you something you should chew on. — You want to catch the wild monkey, you got to climb up the tree. — F'shtast?

SAM. *(nodding, not sure that he does)* Yes.

BUBBIE. This is Isabelle I'm talkin' here, Sam. This one you gotta be smart to catch. She's got too many fellas chasing after her. It makes her dizzy. She doesn't know which one to take.

SAM. I can understand that.

(doorbell)

BUBBIE. *(Glances over at the door, but doesn't move to answer it.*) You want more tea, Sam?

SAM. No thank you.

BUBBIE. Some honey cake — yes?

SAM. No thanks.

(doorbell)

SAM. Aren't you going to answer that?

BUBBIE. Ah — it's the vilde chi-ah — they should all drop dead.

SAM. But you should at least look. *(BUBBIE goes to the door, looks through the peephole, returns to the table where she begins to butter a slice of bread.)*

(doorbell)

SAM. Who is it?

BUBBIE. Henka.

SAM. Mrs. Mandelbaum?

BUBBIE. *(taking a big bite from the bread)* Yeah.

(doorbell and knocks)

SAM. Aren't you going to let her in?

BUBBIE. Who invited her?

(furious knocking)

HANNAH. *(off)* Ida! Open up!

BUBBIE. Such eyes she's got — she saw you through the walls—

(more knocks)

BUBBIE. Okay, okay, okay. *(She opens the door.)*

(HANNAH enters, redfaced.)

HANNAH. Ida, what's the matter with you? I'm ringing and ringing, she sits and eats. Already I could have been shot twice, chopped up in little pieces and stuffed in the incinerator.

BUBBIE. Not so fast, Henka, they couldn't get all of you in so quickly.

HANNAH. Your jokes I can live without. *(Sees SAM, pretends surprise.)* Look who's here! And nobody tells Hannah nothin'. *(waving a finger)* Hanky panky.

SAM. Nothing is going on, Mrs. Mandelbaum. I'm just paying a visit.

HANNAH. So where does Hannah fit in? She's outside in the hallway, bleeding — and you're making big plans without me. Sammy, Idela, you hurt my feelings very deep down.

BUBBIE. You should go work for J. Edgar Hoover, Hannah. He's here two minutes, BOOM, you're in the house. — She's afraid she won't make the money on the shidah. Don't worry. Something sweet happens, you'll get your money. Sam is an honest boy — you shouldn't insult him like this.

HANNAH. Who's insulting? I just come by to say howyado. — Nu? Isabelle, she's still alone?

BUBBIE. Like a stone. She's a very particular person, what can you do?

HANNAH. I don't wish no one to be alone.

BUBBIE. *(nodding)* I been alone for fourteen years since my Sidney died. And I know. To zine alain is a sickness.

HANNAH. Sickness? — Za *disease!*

SAM. Some people enjoy being by themselves.

BUBBIE & HANNAH. *(together)* NO!

SAM. It could be. *(BUBBIE & HANNAH sandwich him in.)* It could be.

HANNAH. So maybe you want to be alone for the rest of your life?

BUBBIE. He wants the best, Hannah — he wants my Isabelle — Can you blame him?

SAM. Thank you for the kugel, Mrs. Kantor — I've got to get back to the store.

HANNAH. Wait — wait. You can walk me back to my bench.

BUBBIE. Sam. *(She stops him.)* I can't promise no promises — I do what I can. *(He starts out with HANNAH.)* Sam. Sammy. In 1920 — three proposals of marriage. Mishka Lebner. Solomon Zlotin. Tevye Fruchman. One, two, three. What can I say? They all wanted me.

(Lights dim to evening as BUBBIE locks door, crosses to the window, where she sits on her stool, sewing.)

BUBBIE. Nem. Nem de scissors.

(IZZY enters and hands her the scissors. She is wearing the Stetson.)

IZZY. *(sitting   at   the   table   and   sewing)* You shouldn't sew by that light. It's not good for you.

BUBBIE. Orders she's giving me. She walks around all day in the house with a hat on like a general and she's giving me orders. *(IZZY takes off the hat.)* I'll tell you a secret, I got eyes like a hawk. Like an elephant never forgets.

IZZY. Come sit by the light if you're going to sew.

BUBBIE. No, I got plenty light from the windows — so nice and clean from the pickleman.

IZZY. *(looking up from her sewing)* What? What do you mean?

BUBBIE. He came today. He washed my windows.

IZZY. He washed your windows?

BUBBIE. While he was here. Why not. Let him give me a hand. It's a mitzvah.

IZZY. What did he want?

BUBBIE. He wants to get next to you, what else?

IZZY. What did you say?

BUBBIE. I told him to stop dreaming — but first I let him wash the windows. *(looking up at the window)* He made a nice job.

IZZY. What else did he say?

BUBBIE. What's to say? — Henka's got plenty girls for him, he's not going to bother you no more.

IZZY. *(pause)* I feel like I should at least thank him.

BUBBIE. What for?

IZZY. The hat.

BUBBIE. Forget it.

IZZY. It's a very nice hat.

BUBBIE. Wear it in the best of health.

IZZY. Probably very expensive.

BUBBIE. He won't starve.

IZZY. It's the only polite thing to do.

BUBBIE. So what do you want from me?

IZZY. Maybe you could ask Mrs. Mandelbaum for his address — or — maybe he could call me. — It's okay. She can give him my number. I don't mind. — And he can call me so I can thank him properly — Okay?

BUBBIE. Yeah, yeah.

IZZY. Will you do it?

BUBBIE. I'll do it, I'll do it.

IZZY. You promise?

BUBBIE. Please! Let me live.

IZZY. I just want to be polite. I should at least thank him.

BUBBIE. Believe me, when Henka pulled him out of here today she was already painting lovely pictures. She's got lots of other girls. She's not in business to joke around. When it comes to love, these are serious people, these Jews.

(Blackout. Lights up on bench. IZZY crosses down to the bench, sits perched on the back, holding the hat.)

IZZY. This is how I see it. — He's on his way to the pickle stand, he passes the hat shop — he stops, he looks in the window, he thinks about it a minute— *(pause)* He gives his head a little shake, he moves on — A block later, he screeches to a halt, turns around, *rushes* back to the store and pulls Finkle away from his sardine sandwich for a full consultation..... "What do you think, Finkle? This is a good one? It's got to be the best. Your number one best. She should look at this hat and know that I am a sincere fellow — not to be taken lightly. — She should know I got style, I got taste — I got class. — No, don't show me the bargains! I'm not interested in bargains. I don't care what it costs. This is the hat for the girl I see whenever I close my eyes. This is the hat for the girl who sings to me in all my waking dreams."

(She puts the hat on and jumps off the bench and into the bookstore as the lights come up. IZZY is at the shelf, her back to the door. SAM enters.)

SAM. Fits. Fits nicely. Very good.

IZZY. *(She recognizes the voice, turns, startled.)* Thank you.

SAM. A good guess, hm?

IZZY. Almost as if I were there in the store with you.

SAM. You were. *(Pause. He looks around the shop.)* This is very comfortable. Very inviting. Not like the big book stores. They're starting to feel like supermarkets. — I can see how it must be a pleasant place to work.

IZZY. Yeah, it's pretty relaxed.

SAM. *(pause)* It was strange for you — meeting me like that at your Bubbie's—

IZZY. Yeah.

SAM. With Mrs. Mandelbaum selling me like a used car.

IZZY. She has some technique.

SAM. But she's a determined lady. I've got to give her credit.

IZZY. Has she introduced you to a lot of women?

SAM. No — you're the first. But she's been after me a long time to meet some of her "clients" as she calls them. Always with the pictures, the stories, the promises.... But when she showed me this one, I finally said, yes, Mrs. Mandelbaum— *(He takes the photo from his wallet.)*

IZZY. *(looking at the photo)* Where did she get this? — They really went to work, didn't they?

SAM. *(Looks over her shoulder at the picture.)* Yes, Mrs. Mandelbaum, this one I'll meet.

IZZY. *(Turns to SAM and lets herself be drawn in — then pulls away.)* You mean you didn't hire her?

SAM. No, no — she's a very active promoter — ze hut mir ein g'vegelt— She makes package deals.

IZZY. Oh, I didn't realize—

SAM. Yes — she grabs one from here, one from there, puts them in the same room and sees what happens.

IZZY. Like a blind date.

SAM. No, not exactly blind — I've been aware of you for quite a while.

IZZY. Oh?

SAM. For almost two years now — I've seen you in the neighborhood — on the benches with your Bubbie. Every now and then.

IZZY. I don't remember seeing you.

SAM. Once, I thought about following you into the building and getting in the elevator with you, just to have a reason to say, hello, excuse me, would you please push number ten — I've been aware of you for quite a while.

(TYLER enters.)

TYLER. Well, there she is, the midnight caller.

IZZY. It wasn't that late— Can I help you with something?

TYLER. I thought we could have that talk — can you get away?

IZZY. No — no I can't.

TYLER. Well, another time.

IZZY. Please.

TYLER. *(turning to SAM)* Don't I know you?

SAM. Yes. Sam Posner. I took a course from you at City College. Couple of years back.

TYLER. You have the beard then?

SAM. No.

TYLER. You brought in the monologues. Tales from the lower east side kind of thing, right?

SAM. That's right.

TYLER. You ever do anything with them?

SAM. You mean publish? — No.

TYLER. You should. They're charming.

SAM. Thank you.

TYLER. See you, Izzy — great hat. *(TYLER exits. IZZY turns to SAM.)*

(Blackout. Lights up on the bench. HANNAH sits in her office, watching her constituency pass by.)

HANNAH. Sam, Sammy — where are you going? Come, sit a minute.

SAM. Hello, Mrs. Mandelbaum.

HANNAH. Where are you going in such a hurry? — Please, make me happy. Sit a minute. *(He does.)* You want my advice, Sam. You need to be a gambler. You were always stuck up with me — you wouldn't give me a chance. This is only the first one you meet. Come, let me introduce you to some more. Lovely girls. I got plenty. Trust me. *(She waves to someone across the park.)* Sophie Levine. She wants me to find someone for her little Marcie. *(She smiles warmly and waves again.)* Three hundred pounds ain't so easy to fit.

SAM. Listen, Mrs. Mandelbaum, I think you should know — I don't want to do this behind your back — I'm seeing Isabelle.

HANNAH. Oh yeah?

SAM. It's just a date. There's nothing for you to get excited about.

HANNAH. I'm very glad you had the decency to tell me. In my business, it's very easy for people to walk all over me. After all, do I ask you to sign a contract? — No. — Do I ask for escalating fees? — No. — It's all a hand-shake.

SAM. But I think it would be better if you let me handle this on my own now.

HANNAH. Of course. Of course.

SAM. Just to keep things simple.

HANNAH. Absolutely. *(pause)* So when is the date?

SAM. Mrs. Mandelbaum—

HANNAH. A simple question.

SAM. Saturday night.

HANNAH. Good, good, you should have a lovely time. You should have much happiness. This is all I wish. *(She looks up alarmed.)* Sam, *please,* start sneezing!

SAM. What?

HANNAH. Please, make like your sneezing! Go on, go on! Take out your hankie — do as I say! Quick! *(He does.)* Good .... good ... louder — Bigger!

SAM. Why am I doing this?

HANNAH. Now blow a little. Blow into the hankie — don't ask questions. This is a red alert. — Good, good. Very good.

SAM. Can I stop now?

HANNAH. *(She nods.)* The danger has passed. Ah .... that Miriam. She chases after me like a hungry dog. She sees you she starts to bark. — But the one thing she don't like is to be near a sneezer. She gets of the bus and walks home ten miles if someone gives a sneeze. I been on the elevator — she stops and shleps up twenty floors if God forbid someone should have a cold.

SAM. That's her in the white jacket?

HANNAH. The white jacket, the white shoes, the white hat — she wants me to find her a man — so healthy, so young, and so rich — he should never get sick, but if he does, he can afford to go away by himself he shouldn't contaminate her. Nu? This is some assignment she gives me. Where is there such a fool?

SAM. *(He rises.)* So long, Mrs. Mandelbaum.

HANNAH. Where you running? Wait — wait — I got something for you. *(She pulls a card out of her bag.)* My brother-in-law Max, a fantastic wholesaler — you heard of Calvin Klein? — Max dresses him. All the machers in the fashion business go to him. The new wave hits Max *before* it hits the beach. You get me? — The well dressed man always has the big advantage, Sam. — Look at history — Fred Astaire, Clark Gable, Allistair Cook — these

are not handsome men. The clothes make them sexy. —
Go to Max, he'll give you the extra something. Believe
me.

*(Blackout. Lights up in the bookstore. Phone rings. Several rings.
IZZY appears from the backroom in complete dishevelment — Her
dress half-on, her long sleeves trailing the floor, she finally lurches
for the phone, juggles it unsuccessfully, finally gets it in her
hands.)*

Izzy. New Day Books. *(Hearing nothing on the other end,
she hangs up.)* Give me a break— *(She turns to the audience,
twisting herself into the stunning dress as she talks.)* I haven't
gotten the system down yet — I've only worn this dress
once before — last year, on my birthday. My friends
Elissa and Billy were taking me out to dinner at the Russian Tea Room — and I thought, why not look like something. — So for the first time in my life, I walked into
Bendels and there it was. — The saleswoman said it had
me written all over it.

(TYLER enters.)

Tyler. Do I see what I think I see? — Has our little
Miss Izzy Goldberg—
Izzy. Grossman.
Tyler. Has our little Miss Isabelle Grossman been
transformed into the image of Grace Kelley at her
dewiest? You look gorgeous!
Izzy. Thanks.
Tyler. You've been hiding all this from your book-

buying public?

Izzy. *Your* book-buying public.

Tyler. Ah — and she's fast too. Come, we must have a drink. You must let me buy you a drink. When are you done here?

Izzy. Six, but—

Tyler. *(Checks his watch.)* Good. Where shall we go? You name it.

Izzy. I'd love to, I'd really love to, but I can't — not tonight.

Tyler. You're a complete mystery to me, my girl. You call me up — badger me for weeks about this interview—

Izzy. I — I didn't badger.

Tyler. *Badger.* And now, here I am, presenting myself to you for the occasion and you say, frig off.

Izzy. Not frig off — just that I have an obligation.

Tyler. What kind of obligation? Who is this obligation?

Izzy. It's a dinner thing.

Tyler. A dinner thing. You're blowing an opportunity that in all likelihood will never come your way again for a dinner thing? Where is the wisdom in that, Ms. Grossman?

Izzy. I don't have any choice.

Tyler. You always have choices, Izzy. When you stop seeing them, you're in real trouble.

Izzy. Couldn't we do this tomorrow?

Tyler. There are no tomorrows. There is only the moment. And it wants to be seized.

Izzy. Are you pressuring me?

TYLER. I most certainly am. — Awwwww — relax. We'll just have a drink. Then you can scoot. — Keep them waiting, Izzy. They like to be kept waiting.

(Blackout. Lights up in BUBBIE's kitchen. The full spread of food on the table. BUBBIE sits in silent horror watching HANNAH systematically devour everything on the table with a steady, well-practiced rhythm. Then standing it no longer.)

BUBBIE. How much you weigh, Henka?

HANNAH. *(not breaking the rhythm of her meal)* I don't know.

BUBBIE. I got a scale.

HANNAH. How old is she — your Isabelle?

BUBBIE. I'll ask her — you got enough to eat there?

HANNAH. Yeah, this is good — Just a snack.

BUBBIE. I wouldn't want you should starve.

HANNAH. Please, don't trouble yourself for me. A bite is good. Until supper.

BUBBIE. Herbie, may he rest in peace, did he ever sit down to eat with you?

HANNAH. What else? — He was my husband.

BUBBIE. All the yentas made blah-blah when he jumped from the sixteenth floor — such a nice, new apartment — why should he want to fly away?

HANNAH. *(still not breaking her rhythm)* He never got a chance to tell me. *(BUBBIE crosses to the window.)* Ida—

BUBBIE. Yeah?

HANNAH. Something's bothering me — I got to know — why are they set up to meet by you tonight? Isabelle's so ashamed to show him where she lives it's so lousy?

BUBBIE.   You stinker — she gives me a little nachas, this is her job. It's such a crime?

HANNAH.   Excuse me for asking. *(pause)* She's coming right from work?

BUBBIE.   Yeah. You don't need to broadcast she works on shabbos.

HANNAH.   Don't worry, I keep secrets like an old cocker keeps a young wife.

BUBBIE.   For my money, she can work on Yom Kippur — honest work is honest work — but I don't want to shake up the little pickleman, f'shtast?

HANNAH.   The little pickleman is already plenty shook.

BUBBIE.   It was the same with me — all the boys, they lost their tongues when they saw me. The poor schmendricks.

HANNAH.   So tell me, Ida, satisfy my curiosity, why did your Isabelle decide to turn around and give him another look. You promise her something nice? Ain't I right? A little gelt maybe?

BUBBIE.   I don't butt in. I don't operate this way.

HANNAH.   So what happened?

(doorbell)

BUBBIE.   In her dreams she saw pickles.

HANNAH.   It's a match.

BUBBIE.   Not so fast. *(She crosses to the door.)*

HANNAH.   It's a match. — I got to admit — sometimes I know what I'm doing in this life.

(BUBBIE looks through the peephole and opens the door, SAM enters. He is wearing an oversized jacket and baggy pants with a cummerbund in the manner of the hip, young Japanese designers. The ensemble looks like it stepped off the cover of GQ. Wearing it, SAM, however, does not. The total effect on him is ludicrous. BUB-BIE does not move.)

HANNAH. *(Rises from the table and crosses to him.)* Sammy, Sammy. Come. Let's take a look. Ohhh la la — I don't know what to say. You take my breath and throw it away. *(She grabs his hand.)* Walk around, show it off. Let me see. *(SAM walks around the kitchen area, avoiding eye contact with both women.)* Very nice. Very nice. You look like a million. Don't let anybody tell you different.

BUBBIE. Who is the thief sold you these schmataz?

SAM. Max.

BUBBIE. Max?

SAM. Mrs. Mandelbaum's brother-in-law.

BUBBIE. I gotta hand it to you, Henka — you get them coming and going.

HANNAH. You think I get something from this? Not a penny. Not a dime. It's part of my job to know fashion. You got to package what you sell. Right, Sam?

BUBBIE. Sammy, you look like you missed the boat back to Pinsk — you understand what I'm saying? — This is not the way educated people dress.

HANNAH. *(pulling SAM away from her)* Leave him alone. Stop criticizing. You look terrific, Sammy. Take it from me. I know what's what with young people. Isabelle will like it. This is all that matters. What's in the bags?

SAM. Mrs. Mandelbaum, what are you doing here?

HANNAH. I'm a sucker for romance— This is my fate.

SAM. Mrs. Kantor — for you. *(He hands her a gift-wrapped box.)* And this is for Isabelle. *(He places a large bouquet of flowers wrapped in paper on the table.)*

HANNAH. Gold. Pure gold. The boy is gold — what did I tell you?

SAM. Aren't you going to open it, Mrs. Kantor?

BUBBIE. Now?

SAM. Please.

BUBBIE. *(She opens the package in her usual careful manner, untying the knots, winding the string, folding the paper, finally removing a bottle of schnapps from the box. As she pulls the bottle out:)* Now you're talking. Let's have a drink, Sammy. What do you say. *(She brings the glasses to the table.)*

SAM. Shouldn't we wait for Isabelle?

BUBBIE. She only drinks milk. Come. *(BUBBIE pours two very full glasses and one half full which she gives to HANNAH.)*

HANNAH. *(as BUBBIE pours)* Sam, it's driving me crazy — I'm looking at you and I'm thinking — who could it be you remind me of dressed up so beautiful like this—

SAM. I can't help you with that one, Mrs. Mandelbaum — I feel like I'm breaking new ground here.

HANNAH. *Vincent Price!* — Vincent Price in The House of Wax!!! ... oh, what a heartbreaker, huh?

BUBBIE. *(holding up the glass for a toast)* Good health, long life, and a heart full of happiness. *(All three clink glasses.)*

ALL. A-main. *(They all drink up, both BUBBIE and HANNAH draining their glasses quickly.)*

HANNAH. Ah! This is what I needed. Thank you, darling. *(She kisses SAM on the cheek.)* Oy! A zees kite!! — So where are you taking the date?

SAM. I thought I'd let Isabelle decide.

HANNAH. Sammy, something wrong? You look a little green.

BUBBIE. Of course he's green. That's some first class garbage you put him in.

SAM. Maybe I should go home and change. It wouldn't take a minute. I'm just around the corner. When Isabelle comes you can tell her I'm on my way, all right?

HANNAH. Don't listen to her. You look fine. Max gave you a good price? You told him you came from me?

SAM. Yes, Mrs. Mandelbaum.

(Phone rings.)

BUBBIE. *(Crosses to answer it.)* Hello — who's there? — Isabelle — you all right?! — I can't hear you — —What? Where are you? — ohhhh — *(spits)* Ptu! You scared me — So why aren't you here, people are waiting .... I don't like this. This I don't like. You make a date to be with someone, you don't mix it up. — So what time you come? Ach — you're some criminal. Here, talk to Sam. He's the lost one. *(She motions to SAM to take the phone.)*

SAM. Isabelle? You're not coming? .... Oh, yes? — Yes ... of course. This sounds important. Certainly. Please, don't rush. We'll wait. We're all relaxed. Anytime with your Bubbie is a good time. — — I understand ..... Goodbye. *(He hangs up.)* I understand.

(Blackout. Lights up in the bench area, now transformed into a banquette with the addition of a long table, pillows, wine glasses, wine bottle, etc.)

IZZY. You put on a new hat, you become a new person.

TYLER. Pickles.

IZZY. Pickles.

TYLER. *(putting down his glass and examining the bottle from which he has been pouring)* I don't think this bottle goes down as well as the first — shall we go back to the other?

IZZY. I think it's quite good.

TYLER. You're sure. It seems a little vapid to me.

IZZY. *(tasting carefully)* I think it's got a lot to say.

TYLER. *(He refills her glass.)* — So — the arranger — what's her name?

IZZY. Henka.

TYLER. Henka — does she come along with you?

IZZY. God, I hope not — that would be real agony. She likes to cozy up real close and breathe into your face. "Isabelle — I got something for you —" *(She moves nose to nose into TYLER.)* It's all very confidential. Anything you want to know about anybody. She's got all the stats. She's a walking *Who's What* of the entire Jewish population of the lower east side.

TYLER. Well, I think it's charming — your Jewish heritage — the way you're experiencing it — up close. But isn't this guy pretty serious?

IZZY. I suppose.

TYLER. And are your intentions honorable?

IZZY. I won't hurt anyone.

Tyler. He'll just move on to the next prospect.

Izzy. Exactly.

Tyler. Then why see him at all?

Izzy. My grandmother set it up. She wants to dance at my wedding. Sometimes I think that's what keeps her alive, that ambition.

Tyler. And you — what's your ambition?

Izzy. I don't have any. That's against the law in this town, I know.

Tyler. There are millions of people, Izzy, who go through their lives thinking they can't have what they want because they're simply afraid to ask for it — I don't mean to sound so glib about it — I steer as far from the hot tub mentality as I can, it's just that I do believe in searching for, identifying and putting your hands on — what you really want. *(His hands move under the table.)*

Izzy. I never would have imagined that kind of straight agression from what I've read — from — from your work.

Tyler. Oh *no*. No, it's not aggression. It's focus. It's the ability to fantasize in the broader dimensions that I cultivate. Certainly you've seen that much. If you've read my books — and I assume you have. *(She nods.)* Then you've seen a pattern of growth — towards this one kernel of insight — to see clearly is to perceive the riches of one's own true desires — stripped clean of the burdens of shame, humility, self-doubt. — That's one of the reasons I admire you, actually.

Izzy. Me?

Tyler. Yes. The way you've been zeroing in on me — saturating yourself with information — collecting all the right materials to script the fantasies that have carried you here. Now. To this moment. We aren't here to discuss my work, are we?

Izzy. I guess not.

Tyler. We're here because we need each other. And we have the guts — yes, the guts to say so. *(He kisses her firmly on the lips.)* I want you in my life, Isabelle Grossman.

Izzy. *(weakly)* You don't even know me.

Tyler. *(He kisses her again.)* But I need you. My assistant ran out on me today. She got a Fullbright — right under my nose she applied — Anyway, the position is wide open — not much money, but lots of stimulation. Do you type?

Izzy. Yes.

Tyler. Well, there we are.

Izzy. Where?

Tyler. Don't miss this one, Isabelle, don't wake yourself up in the middle of your juiciest dream.

Izzy. I haven't been dreaming about being your secretary.

Tyler. *Assistant.* Big difference. You get to do research, organize my calendar, meet my friends, type historic literary correspondence — and most important of all — learn. I'll give you time — real time to work on your own stuff. I'll even read it. *(He picks the hat up and puts it on her head.)* I love that on you. Could become kind of a signature thing. It's never too early to find your image— *(He kisses her fingers, one at a time.)* You're such a complete woman-child. That's how I'll always think of you — Is that offensive? — I'm sorry, but you're so open and needy and caring and it's a very appealing combination. *(He downs his glass, leans back and smiles easily.)* And now I think it's time to take me home.

Izzy. There's an old Yiddish expression my Bubbie taught me — quite appropriate here— *(She rises.)* Kush mir in tuchas. *(Blackout.)*

(Lights up in BUBBIE's apartment. She sleeps soundly in her chair, clutching a newspaper in her lap. SAM sits at the kitchen table, writing something on a pad. He has changed into the same outfit he wore in Act I. He looks up as the key turns in the lock. IZZY enters.)

Izzy. I didn't think you'd still be here.

Sam. *(rising)* I said I would wait. I wait. You got to see I'm a man you can trust.

Izzy. Has she been sleeping long?

Sam. Half hour maybe — Do you think we should put her to bed?

Izzy. No, that's all right. Before I go, I'll help her up.

Sam. It was worth it to stay late? You got everything done at your store?

Izzy. No.

Sam. You shouldn't work so hard. You got to dance between work — a little dance, a little work. The perfect sandwich. With a pickle thrown in.

Izzy. I didn't have to stay late at work.

Sam. I have to tell you confidentially — she wasn't disappointed you didn't show up right away. After Mrs. Mandelbaum left we really had some fun. We got a good start on the bottle. *(Picks up the nearly empty bottle of schnapps.)* Did she ever show you the one where she dances with her hands in the air and jiggles her muscles? —Unbelievable — and another good one — she takes my glass to pour in some more, she gives it back to me, I look I see she adds ice cubes, very peculiar since I make a big point of saying, please Mrs. Kantor, no ice. I look again — I see it's not ice, it's her teeth! She took out her teeth and put them in the glass!

Izzy. Don't you want to know why I was late?

Sam. Would it make me happy to know this?

Izzy. I don't think so.

Sam. Then why should I ask for unhappiness?

Izzy. You're very wise.

Sam. It's not wisdom that's talking, Isabelle. *(pause)* So, where would you like to go now? You got someplace in mind maybe?

Izzy. No — not really.

Sam. Okay. Then …. if you're hungry we could get some dinner — it's kind of late, but I know a wonderful place stays open, should be still serving—

Izzy. No, thanks, I'm not hungry.

Sam. Or — we could go dancing. Do you like to dance? Not that I claim to be the most wonderful dancer, but my friend Lenny Kaplan just opened a new nightclub on Rivington. He's always asking me to come. If you like...

Izzy. Do you mind, could we just stay here for a while?

Sam. Sure … sure.

Izzy. I just need to settle down for a few minutes.

SAM. Sure ... you been running around.

IZZY. Yeah.

SAM. So .... we'll sit a while. *(Pause. He holds up the bottle.)* Would you like a taste? There's plenty left. It will feel good.

IZZY. Okay.

SAM. *(He pours a small glass for IZZY and more for himself. Laughing to himself.)* Right in the glass she put her teeth... *(They toast.)*

TOGETHER. L'chaim.

IZZY. Do you smell something?

SAM. Like what?

IZZY. Kind of sweet — kind of like vanilla, I think.

SAM. It is vanilla. *(He holds up his hands.)* I soak them in vanilla and milk to take away the pickle smell. It's an occupational hazard, I guess you call it.

IZZY. Well, it works.

SAM. Does it bother you?

IZZY. No, no no ... not at all. It's nice.

SAM. It's what my father did. Whenever I smelled that sweet cloud, I knew he was home.

IZZY. What was his name?

SAM. Jacob. *Jake the Comedian.* "A Joke and a Pickle All for A Nickle." He had an act — like a real act, he did every Sunday. — He was just like his idol, a real Milton Berle.

IZZY. And do you still give away jokes with your pickles?

SAM. Me? — No, no — it's turned around with me... The customers give *me* the show. I'm a listener for them. I got customers coming to me with all kinds of interesting lives turned upside down.

Izzy. So what do they tell you? What do they talk about?

Sam. Oh, everything you can imagine and more. — With the old ones it's like a list ... what happened, what didn't happen, what *should* have happened — A memory from childhood — something small that tumbled out of a dream — and they got to talk about it to make it real, you know?

Izzy. Yeah, I know what you mean ... I come down here every week, go through the same routines with Bubbie, listen to her tell me the same stories over and over again. — It's almost like a ceremony, isn't it?

Sam. *(He nods.)* This is the most wonderful thing you can do for yourself, Isabelle, to be with her like this. You'll learn plenty from her. Your Bubbie knows how to fight.

Izzy. You saw the muscle.

Sam. I saw — you should write down what she tells you. All of it. These are diamonds she gives you. — I keep a little notebook for this purpose. *(He picks it up from the table.)* I put it down whenever the idea is clear to me. I put it down. And questions, too. When they are clearly in my mind, I like to see them on the page. I leave room for the answers. Here, you see — this is a question I have been looking at — "How do I talk to Isabelle?" *(He puts the pad down and paces about the kitchen.)* It's hard this business of getting acquainted. You want to say the right thing. You want to show the other person the best you got. Like in the market when I go to buy the cukes — They got the samples on display — always the tastiest looking, perfect sizes. One summer when I was a boy my Papa got me a job working at the wholesale produce market so I would know the other side of the business better — also to see the world a little, I think— And the guys who run the stands they put these samples out for each kind of vegetable and fruit they're selling — so you know what you're getting when you buy your bushel basket. And these samples they call flash. And at the end of the day when the market's closing down, the boss comes around and says, "okay, work the flash!" That means — you can sell it, you can let it go, the flash, the best stuff you got..... I want very much to show you the best I got, Isabelle. Please let me do that. *(IZZY crosses to the sink with some dishes from the table.)* Maybe I talked too much — but I been saving up.

Izzy. It's a pleasure to hear you talk, Sam. It's the best talk I've heard in a long time.

Sam. Well .... I'm sure this isn't true, but — you make me very happy by saying it.

Izzy. *(pause)* Sam — I don't know what I'm doing.

Sam. What do you mean?

Izzy. I have no business wasting your time.

Sam. I don't understand.

Izzy. I don't belong here.

Sam. Where is here?

Izzy. You know what I mean.

Sam. You think it's so small, my world? You think it's so provincial? — You think it defines me? — Is that the problem?

Izzy. Sam ... I'm confused about a lot of things, but I do know that I don't want to hurt you. — I wish I could turn myself into what you're looking for, into who you think I am, but I can't...

SAM. Excuse me, but how do you know what I'm looking for? What angel have you been talking to who gives away these secrets? Do you know I was so full of happiness to know I was going to see you today, to be in the same room with you, I made a special brocha for the occasion — I said the prayer for the planting of new trees — don't ask me why. Isabelle, I don't know why these things come to pass, but this is it. This is all my heart on the table in front of you. *(He crosses to her and kisses her. It is a short, gentle kiss, but it leaves IZZY spinning.)* It's all right for me to kiss you like this?

IZZY. It's all right. *(She falls into his arms and a long kiss.)*

BUBBIE. *(Several seconds into the second kiss, she opens her eyes fully and sits up in the chair. She stares at SAM and IZZY, adjusts herself noisily, then shouts:)* WHAT TIME IS IT? *(They part, startled.)* You let me sleep so long in the chair I don't know even where I am! — Who is this man? What is he doing in my house?

IZZY. *(Crosses to BUBBIE.)* Shhhhhhh, don't yell. We didn't want to wake you. You were sleeping so peacefully. This is Sam. You remember Sam.

BUBBIE. *(Stares at him blankly.)* No.

IZZY. He's a new friend of mine. Mrs. Mandelbaum introduced us. You remember.

BUBBIE. No.

IZZY. Okay, okay.... *(She pats her. To SAM.)* Maybe the drink— *(to BUBBIE)* I'll get your bed ready. Relax. I'll be right back. *(She exits.)*

BUBBIE. *(Pause. Continues to stare blankly at SAM, motions him over with a wiggle of her finger. She inspects him closely. SAM shuffles uncomfortably. Suddenly, she gives him a good jab in the side)* You're some big time operator, Sammy. *(motioning for him to pull a chair over)* A little story — when I was a girl, such a thing to look at, I walked always with my thumbs hidden like this — to keep away the bad eyes. A fellow named Shiah, a tailor's son, comes to me. Ida, he says, Ida, look at me, I'm falling in pieces. My life is over if you won't take me. I'm going into the East River. This will be my grave. He was a clean little fellow with spectacles. A good family, but he wasn't nothing to me. Another boy who comes to look at the beautiful flower — that's all. But he sits himself down in my Aunt Bessie's kitchen and he says, "I won't move. I won't crawl an inch until you say yes. I'm stuck here like a piece of furniture."

SAM. So what did you do?

BUBBIE. I married him, what else? — I didn't want to bother poor Bessela. She had enough troubles with her lousy teeth. And in the end it was good. — When someone wanted me so much he was ready to make a fool of himself, it was easy to see he would be good to me. — Sammy, I want to dance. Yes? You'll dance with me at the wedding? I'll make some nice cakes. You'll buy the schnapps. We'll have a good time.

SAM. We'll see, Bubbie — we'll see.

BUBBIE. Like a piece of furniture — you hear me!

(IZZY enters. BUBBIE resumes her dazed expression.)

IZZY. Okay, it's ready. Let's go. *(She helps BUBBIE up gently by the elbow.)*

BUBBIE. *(as she rises slowly)* Oy, vays mir — not so fast — don't push me. I got to go slow — oy, such a pain my enemies should know—

IZZY. Where?

BUBBIE. In the legs. In the knees. Come, walk with me. Bring the alcohol. *(She turns back and points at SAM.)* You know this fellow? Who is this man?

IZZY. This is Sam, Bubbie.

BUBBIE. He's keeping company with you?

IZZY. That's right.

BUBBIE. Oh yeah? *(She puts her face closely into SAM's.)* He looks okay. *(She shuffles on a few more steps, then turns back to SAM.)* She's some beauty, huh? Not like her old Bubbie broken down. *(turning to IZZY)* He takes you home tonight?

IZZY. Yes, Bubbie.

BUBBIE. You like him?

IZZY. Yes, Bubbie.

BUBBIE. He's a Jew?

IZZY. I think so.

BUBBIE. You'll bring him with you next time you come?

IZZY. I'll bring him with me next time I come.

BUBBIE. He'll buy me some Cherry Herring? I love Cherry Herring.

SAM. It would be a pleasure, Mrs. Kantor.

BUBBIE. Come, Sam, take my arm — You can touch me. It's all right. One hundred twenty pounds pure gold. That's me. Come, come, children .... let's put the Bubbie to bed. *(They turn and exit together.)*

CURTAIN

YIDDISH WORDS AND PHRASES

CHARACTER	PAGE	PHRASE	TRANSLATION
BUBBIE.	9	Oy!	Exclamation of alarm
IZZY.	10	Bubbie	Grandmother
BUBBIE.	10	Vas	What
BUBBIE.	14	Meshugah	Crazy
BUBBIE.	15	Koot-sehs	Turds
BUBBIE.	15	Pas-kootz-vehs	Despicable people (female)
BUBBIE.	16	Tagelah	Pastry: honeyed balls of dough woven through with raisins and nuts
BUBBIE.	16	Shadkhn	Marriage broker
BUBBIE.	18	Mine ainical	My grand child
BUBBIE.	18	Alta cockers	Old people (derogatory)
BUBBIE.	30	Hocking me a chineick	Annoying me (literally: banging a teapot at me)
HANNAH, SAM.	31	Zi ge zunt	Go in good health; be well
HANNAH.	33	Vus tuht seh	What's happening? or How's it going?
HANNAH.	34	Tzimis	(to make a) fuss, a big deal
BUBBIE.	35	Nem	Take
BUBBIE.	35	Hundred ts-vansig	One hundred and twenty

BUBBIE.	36	Schmendrick	Poor soul
BUBBIE.	38	Oy gevalt	Exclamation of surprise
BUBBIE, SAM.	39	Zere gut	Very good
SAM.	39	Shule	Synagogue
SAM.	39	Hassid	A member of the orthodox Jewish Hassidic sect
BUBBIE.	40	Kugel	Pudding
BUBBIE.	40	(song)	See pages 85 & 86 for translation and music
BUBBIE.	40	Ofen Pribitzik	The title of a song
BUBBIE.	40	Der alta mahn	The title of a song, "The Old Man"
BUBBIE.	40	De kugeleh song	The title of the song about kugel that she has just sung
BUBBIE.	42	F'shtast	(You) understand?
BUBBIE.	43	Vilde chi-ah	Literally, wild beasts— (in usage has come to mean the young criminal population that preys on the urban elderly)
BUBBIE.	44	Shidah	Marriage arrangement
BUBBIE.	45	Zine alain	Live alone
BUBBIE.	46	Mitzvah	Good deed

SAM.	49	Ze hut mir ein g'vegelt	She inveigled me.
HANNAH.	52	Shleps	drags
HANNAH.	52	Nu?	So? / What do you think?
HANNAH.	52	Machers	Big shots
BUBBIE.	55	Yentas	Gossips
BUBBIE.	56	Nachas	Pleasure felt through pride in a loved one
BUBBIE.	56	Shabbos	The sabbath
HANNAH.	56	Gelt	Money
BUBBIE.	57	Schmataz	Rags
ALL.	58	A-main	Ahmen
HANNAH.	59	Zees kite	Sweetness
IZZY.	63	Kush mir in tuchas	Kiss my ass.
SAM, IZZY.	65	L'chaim	To life
SAM.	68	Brocha	Prayer
BUBBIE.	69	Vays mir	Woe is me.

PROP LIST

SET PROPS:

Bubbie's:

>   Kitchen table w/4 chairs
>   Refrigerator (opens from the left)
>   Stove
>   Counter (built)
>   Kitchen sink (cupboards built)
>   Radiator
>   Window (built)
>   Stool
>   Door (built)

Bookstore:

>   Bookcase (built)
>   Counter (built)
>   Stool
>   Door (built)

Park:

>   Park bench (built)
>   Tree w/gate

DRESSING:

Bubbie's:

>   Silverware
>   Glasses

Cutting knives
Teapot
Tea kettle
Pot holders
Dish towels
Napkins in holder
Plates
Tea cups
Bags
Cooking utensils
Assorted goods in refrigerator & cupboards
Phone — black, desk, dial
Dish soap
Trash can w/liners
Mirror inside cupboard
Saucepan
Sugar bowl
Trivets
Dish drain

Bookstore:
New, hardcover books
Cash register
Magazines
Clipboard w/lists
Pencils
Metal file box w/3x5 cards
Desk calendar
Phone — pushbutton
New York Book Reviews

Personal Props:
BUBBIE: 40 $1 bills

TYLER: Mechanical pencil, towel

SAM: Handkerchief, wallet w/photo, notebook w/pen

HANNAH: Purse w/notebook & business cards

CONSUMABLES:
Second Avenue Deli:
    Kugel
    Bread

Store bought:
    Coffee
    Tea
    Milk
    Sweet & low
    Cookies
    Pencil lead
    Jars of pickles, kraut and tomatoes
    Flowers

Made:
    Blintzes

HAND PROPS

Scene 1 BUBBIE's
    Tweezers
    Coffee
    Coffee pot
    Coffee cup & saucer
    2 short coffee glasses
    Bread & cookies on plate w/knife
    Napkins in holder
    $40 in ones in pouch (P)
    I's purse w/keys, sunglasses and wallet
    Small plate w/bread
    2 small plates
    Cafe au lait in saucepan
    2 tall glasses
    Bag of food in fridge
    Foil-wrapped snack in fridge

Scene 2 BOOKSTORE
    Phone
    "Freefall"
    I's glasses

Scene 3 PARK
    I's purse w/sunglasses
    H's purse
    Shopping bag w/tagalech

Scene 4 BOOKSTORE
    Index card file
    "Freefall"
    I's purse
    I's glasses
    Dental floss
    Mechanical pencil (P)

Scene 5 BUBBIE's
    Iron
    Pillow case

Scene 6 BOOKSTORE
    New York book review
    I's glasses
    Index card file box

Scene 7 BUBBIE's
    3 teacups & saucers
    Kettle
    Tea glass
    3 plates w/blintzes
    3 forks
    Small plate
    Posner's shopping bag 4/4 jars (off R)
    Photograph (off L)
    2 flat hot pads
    Teapot
    Napkins in holder

Scene 8 BOOKSTORE
    Phone receiver
    Towel (P)
    Index cards w/dialogue on
    Bookstore phone

Scene 9 PARK
    I's purse
    H's purse w/notebook

Scene 10 BUBBIE's
    Wrapped package w/choc. cake in box, Stetson in hat box (off R)
    Clipboard w/pencil (off R)
    ID (off R)
    Alcohol (off L)
    Sharp knife
    Glass & plate
    Mirror in cupboard

ACT TWO

Scene 1 BUBBIE's
    Pole w/rags on end (off R)
    Kugel in pan
    Hot pads
    Trivet
    Plate w/bread
    2 plates
    Fork
    Teapot

Tea
2 tea glasses
Spatula
Knife

Scene 2 BUBBIE's
Sewing
Sewing (off R)
Scissors (off R)
Stetson (off R)

Scene 2A BOOKSTORE
Stetson
Sam's wallet w/photo (P)
Pile of books
Index cards
Stack of magazines

Scene 3 PARK
Handkerchief (P)
S's notebook (P)
Hannah's purse w/notebook & business cards (P)

Scene 4 BOOKSTORE
Phone

Scene 5 BUBBIE's
Shopping bag w/wrapped flowers, wrapped
schnapps
3 small glasses
Phone

Vase
Cookies in pan
Trivet
Hot pads

Scene 6 RESTAURANT
Cafe table w/tablecloth
2 wine glasses ¼ full
1 bottle of white wine ½ full
Stetson
Clutch w/keys

Scene 7 BUBBIE's
Sam's notebook
Alcohol
Stetson
Clutch w/keys
Schnapps bottle
2 glasses

COSTUMES

BUBBIE

I-1	Green plaid dress w/beige apron
I-3	Green plaid dress w/khaki sweater
I-5	Blue dress w/pink apron
I-7	Blue dress
I-10	Blue floral smock
II-1 & 2	Red dress w/grey apron
II-5 & 7	Red dress

Black shoes, wedding band, watch, opaque hose throughout.

ISABELLE

I	Grey tennis togs, w/grey tights, wool socks, hi-top sneakers w/yellow laces, silver earrings, watch, black shoulder bag, barettes
II-2 & 2A	Grey tennis togs, w/yellow tights, wool socks, hi-top sneakers w/white laces, Stetson, watch, silver earrings, barettes, glasses
II-4, 6 & 7	Green dress, crystal earrings, black pumps, Stetson, clutch, barettes, black hose

HANNAH

I-3	Purple dress, beige jacket, brown shoes, brown purse, knee high hose
I-7	Purple skirt, pink blouse, brown shoes, glasses

I-9   Purple skirt, pink blouse, brown shoes, beige jacket, glasses

II-1   Purple dress

II-3   Black dress, beige jacket, brown purse

II-5   Black dress

Brown shoes, pearls, pearl earrings, knee high hose and 4 rings throughout.

SAM

I-7   White shirt, navy cardigan, tweed suit pants, black shoes and socks, blue tie

II-1   Plaid shirt, cotton pants, black belt, black shoes and socks

II-2A&3   Add sweater vest, jacket

II-5   White pants, Star Trek top, scarf, tan boots

II-7   White shirt, tweed suit, green tie, black shoes & socks

Watch worn throughout.

TYLER

I-4   Blue pants, blue jacket, blue belt, striped polo

I-6   Beige chinos, passport shirt, brown belt

I-8   Bathrobe, towel

II-2A   Blue and tan Hawaiian shirt, blue pants

II-4&6   Plaid shirt, brown pants, sportscoat, brown belt

White socks and topsiders worn throughout.

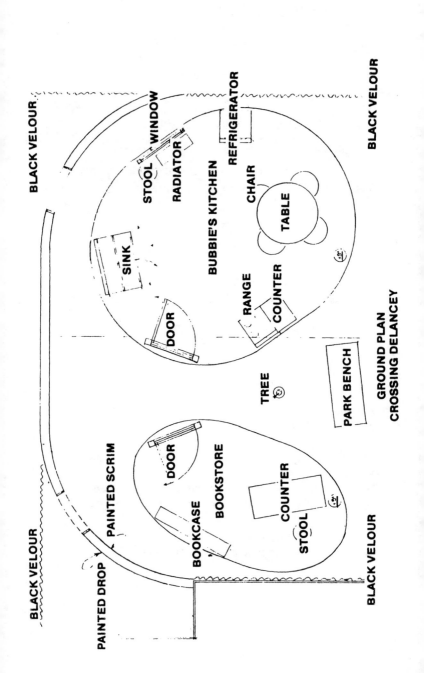

BLACK VELOUR

BLACK VELOUR

BLACK VELOUR

BLACK VELOUR

STOOL WINDOW

RADIATOR

REFRIGERATOR

BUBBIE'S KITCHEN

CHAIR

TABLE

SINK

RANGE

COUNTER

DOOR

GROUND PLAN
CROSSING DELANCEY

TREE

PARK BENCH

PAINTED SCRIM

DOOR

BOOKSTORE

PAINTED DROP

BOOKCASE

COUNTER

STOOL

Kügel Song

HOT A YID AN ID-E-LE HOT ER FUN IR TSU-RIS MACHT SIE OIS A
HÜ-GE-LE TOI-GES OYF HA-PO-RES OY! MEIN MAN! AZ OI VIEL DER
MA-CHES VIF'L DE KÜ-GE-LE HOST MIR HA-PO-HES

Folk Song

HU SU SI DA HOT A BI-LA HU SU SI DA ZHIN-HA MI-LA
CHA-YU ME NA NICH A TIN-KA NE MAN CHAS A NE ME-ZHIN-HA

KUGEL SONG
(with translation)

HOT A YID A YIDELE
(has a Jew a Jewish woman?

HUT ERR FUN IR TSURIS
(has he trouble from her?)

MACHT TSIE OIS A KUGELE
(she made him a pudding)

TAIG ISS OYF KAPOR-RES!
(so awful it could only be used as a sacrifice!)

OY! MEIN MAN! AZ OI VIEL DER MA-CHES
(oh, my man, you should have so many boils)

VIF'L DE KUGELE
(as this pudding)

KOST MIR KAPOKES
(cost me in kopeks)